Flat

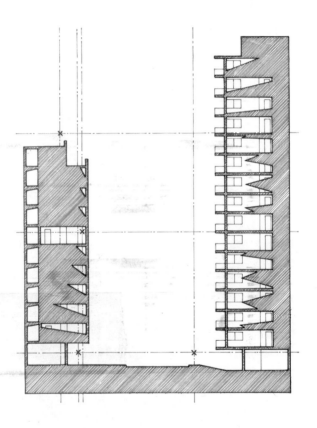

Flat

Mark Macdonald

Arsenal Pulp Press
Vancouver, Canada

FLAT

Copyright © 2000 by Mark Macdonald

SECOND PRINTING / FIRST U.S. EDITION: 2001

ARSENAL PULP PRESS
    103-1014 Homer Street
    Vancouver, BC
    Canada V6B 2W9
    arsenalpulp.com

The publisher gratefully acknowledges the support of the Canada Council for the Arts and the B.C. Arts Council for its publishing program, and the support of the Government of Canada through the Book Publishing Industry Development Program for its publishing activities.

This is a work of fiction. Any resemblance of characters to persons, living or dead, is purely coincidental.

Interior design by Solo
Map and photos by Mark Macdonald
Architectural drawings by David Weir

Printed and bound in Canada

CANADIAN CATALOGUING IN PUBLICATION DATA:
Macdonald, Mark, 1970-

    Flat

    ISBN 1-55152-090-7

I. Title.
PS8575.D6562F52 2000   C813'.6   C00-910820-3
PR9199.3.M31154F52 2000

To Dippy, Lil, & Puss

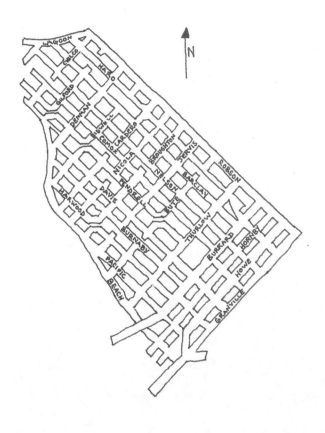

1

#805 – 1461 Harwood Street

In the winter, Apartment 805 is sometimes bathed in the orange light of sunsets. This light is as much a selling point of the apartment as the view or the low rent. Filtering through the horizontal blinds, the rooms are cross-hatched in shadows that move imperceptibly up the walls before dark.

Lit by this impossibly golden glow is the body of J. He is lying like a porn star on the living room futon, legs spread, genitals exposed to the voyeurs across the street. They would think he is asleep until their sticky binoculars passed over the table beside him, picking out the details of spilled pills, and journals and pads filled with frantic notes, sketches, and diagrams. A whisky bottle tipped delicately as if placed there for effect. Perhaps they were the ones who called the cops.

The walls here are entirely covered. He

has collaged a million scraps and postcards, writings, news clippings, paintings, photographs, maps. No one looking for the first time would recognize a pattern, but he knew how to read it all. Drawings of buildings around the West End, with pure, even lines, and from dozens of angles, are stacked neatly beside rows of sagging book cases. Above the couch, above the body, there is a large satellite image of the whole neighbourhood, stolen with care from the city archives.

Somewhere down the hall music is playing. Crows bicker over a pizza crust and pursue each other past the windows. A stack of unopened mail sits on a shelf, just inside the door. Voices from somewhere else, maybe upstairs, filter through the vent above the stove in tinny echoes.

In the bedroom, piles of clean laundry, sorted by colour, are stacked in tidy towers on the bed that has been freshly made, but not slept in. In here, the orange and black lines cast by the sunset are fading. If you lived here, you would know what time it was by where the light fell on the walls. A couple of half-read books beside the bed.

J.'s body looks good in this fading light. One arm lies down alongside him, the other hangs out into the space of the room, the fingers almost flippant, like Adam reaching casually to touch the hand of God. His eyes are open and dry, staring up at the last visible motes of dust that swirl in the twilight. Everything is in its place.

Two Vancouver cops will walk through the front door, turning quickly to spare the aged landlady. The coroner will be called and two days later he will declare a suicide. Someone will call a friend of the tenant because there is no trace of family history or numbers in an address book. The walls and rooms will be cleaned up, and it will become just 805 again, rented once more as an empty space waiting for new histories to develop within. The walls here are strong.

2

#318 – 1235 Nelson Street

*S*ome things happen in life so gradually that you just don't see them until they're new limbs sprouting from your body, fully grown, grasping. The geometry of the world has changed so obviously and so completely that I am ashamed that I only notice now. I remember when the world was curving and fluid, when the repeating patterns of fractals and spirals really mattered. There was a natural grace and beauty to the movement of things. Luscious, innocent, passionate, naïve.

– J.'s notebook

What a fucking nightmare! How is it that a project as big as this can develop for so long, and involve me so much, without my knowledge? This whole world of weirdness was evolving and taking shape and just waiting to burst into my life with one phone call. All the while, I'm living my life, just enjoying myself, taking it easy, dealing with my own shit, basically minding my own business. Who knew one telephone conversation could transform all of that into all of this, whatever the hell this is.

The call came out of the blue, of course. I was certainly not thinking of J. when his landlady rang. I'm sitting there one minute, puttering away in my own little world, and wham: J's dead, they think he killed himself. They can't track any family down, but they found my number at his place and quickly passed the buck. How and where they found my number is still a mystery to me, but suddenly I had this huge responsibility to take care of J's affairs, settle his bills, arrange his funeral, try to find anyone in his family, someone to send all his worldly possessions to, and at the end, try to figure out what the hell happened to make him top himself in the first place. Great.

It's not like J. and I were best friends or anything to begin with. I met him at a party a few years back, and always assumed that many of our mutual friends knew him better than I did. I would see him from time to time on the street, or at the bar, but he never seemed too chummy or anything, just an acquaintance. He certainly never seemed depressed. I'm not sure whether I ever gave him my phone number, but maybe I did. You see, ours was a casual relationship in the extreme.

So I got the phone call. At first I was simply not into it, but I said I'd go and have a look, and see if I could find someone more appropriate to do all this stuff. J's landlady was clearly curious, but she didn't even want to go into his apartment. I was surprised that she bothered knocking on the door, and we waited there self-consciously for a moment, like we didn't want to surprise J. in a state of undress or something. She unlocked the door for me, and sort of just lingered there as I went in and opened the blinds. And standing there, looking around at the mess, the stacks of books and drawings, the pictures all over the walls, the couch where they found his body sprawled out, it began to sink in. This was monumental. This would take days.

There was a smell I won't describe.

The landlady gave me J's keys and mail, and then vanished. I was to simply let her know when everything was out of there, and she would send in the painters and rent the place out as soon as possible. I think it was her first tenant to actually die in the building, so she was quietly freaked out, and she seemed impatient to have the whole presence of J. tidied away. I sat in there alone for hours, just taking it all in. J. was clearly a complicated individual. I hardly knew any- thing about him then, but I was beginning to know him in retrospect.

I put an ad in the papers with my own cash, announcing his death, and posed the question: Is there anyone at all who knew him? A relative? Friends? Not one response came. Apparently he had no lawyer, no fami- ly, he left no will or even a suicide note. The only phone number at all that the police found was mine. Did he know that they would assign me to the project? Was this planned? Did he OD by mistake?

The cops said he took almost a whole bottle of something called "Flutoxocet." Apparently it's an anti-depressant or mood stabilizer or something. He swallowed all these pills with half a litre of fairly good scotch. I found out the brand name, but they wouldn't give me the remains of the actual bottle he was drinking from. I decided that whenever I went back to continue cleaning, I should probably be drinking that scotch. I ended up cleaning in shifts, attacking one room at a time, for fear of becoming too used to being in a dead man's space.

And it was a bizarre little space, too. J. had made a kind of mosaic that covered every inch of wall space in all of the rooms except the bathroom and kitchen. It was constructed out of postcards mostly, but also things cut from magazines and books, photographs he probably took, little fragments of writing, even just words from newspaper headlines. Each tiny piece of paper was stuck up there with little barrels of masking tape. I couldn't see any pattern in the disarray of pictures and words, but I felt compelled to keep them separate. As I spent hours and hours removing the papers, and carefully peeling off the tape loops, I found that in some areas of the flat, there were pictures behind pictures, layers of images and words sometimes four deep. When every last shred of it was down, it filled three fairly big boxes.

The books were all about architecture and engineering, mostly really dull stuff. But tucked away on the shelves were six books he had filled with his own writing. I placed these in the boxes with the things from the walls, intending somehow to go over it all later, maybe try to piece together a picture of his mind. The other stuff would all be divided up for charity. The clothes would go to the Sally Ann, the furniture and dishes would go to the hospice near my place. I would sell the books and anything of value as payment for my time. I felt this would not be too inappropriate; after all, I didn't ask to be the one to make these decisions.

My mind bounced between the project at hand and the utter lack of reason that it should fall on me, of all people, to complete it. Why me? How did I become involved? I found the idea of taking care of all of J.'s loose ends engaging, and somehow rewarding; it might be me, after all, who could take some pride in just helping out. But for what possible reason? I felt that J. had certainly chosen me for the task, but in what capacity, and why? It immediately felt like I was helping out any stranger on the street who might need me. In the end, I wondered if it mattered just how I had become involved with J.'s life – and death – and I wondered if I might not be as arbitrary if I had been in his shoes.

I would come back with a friend's car, and load up all of J.'s stuff, then return and clean the empty space. Damage deposits came to mind, and I didn't want the landlady to get screwed by the situation. It was all going along very rationally. Everything had a place to go to, and the details were being taken care of. J. had one very pathetic-looking jade plant, which I decided to nurse back to health at my place. It was all coming along nicely. Then, and who knows what triggered it, I started to feel my presence here change.

I began to realize that this was really some-one's home. The moldy cottage cheese that I threw out while I was cleaning the fridge had been actually shoppcd for by someone. These were his knives and forks. This was his shaving cream and toothbrush. This was the futon couch where they found him, this exact spot, naked and dead and unknown. I poured more scotch. Who was he?

Expecting, half hoping, to find a cache of dirty magazines or at least a supply of con-doms, I went to work on his bedroom. In his drawers there were only clothes. More clothes, freshly laundered and separated by colour, were stacked neatly like little towers on his bed. Under his bed, there was only one pair of dirty socks. The only thing I found that even approached being suspect was another bottle of Flutoxocet. He must have really liked this stuff. I secreted this untouched supply away with the things I was taking home with me, unsure what I would do with it. At his bedside I found the only two novels in his apartment. *Invisible Cities* by Italo Calvino, and *Exercises in Style* by Raymond Queneau. They would go back to my place.

A picture of someone was beginning to develop in my mind. J. had no apparent sexual outlet, or life, for that matter. He didn't own a stereo or music to play on one. He didn't own a pair of binoculars, which seemed very odd for someone living in an apartment building. I even had a pair, and only lived in a three-storey building. He didn't own anything frivolous, nothing funny, no teddy bear or personally revealing belongings at all. Just lots and lots of pictures and drawings, and maps, and books. It was clear that any effort to truly know about J. would take me through these convoluted papers.

As I packed up the last items that would indicate J. ever lived here, I found the empty space hollow somehow, like the air itself belonged to him, too. These walls were his challenge to cover. This floor knew his footsteps. The water in the tap was intended to wash J. and quench his thirst, but now there was something different. I could feel myself being troubled by this vague emptiness, as if observing from outside. I noticed the way I walked around, heard myself muttering as I lifted the boxes and carried them to the elevator. These were the first indications of my own changed life. They were new and undeveloped, but they were growing.

3

#2401 – 1808 Comox Street

Oh, holy god. I feel like death. My head feels like a ravaged hole. It's always the same the morning after, though I've improved the situation by not letting anyone actually pass out here overnight. It was my birthday yesterday, and birthdays should come with someone to tidy up for you the next day. No one should suffer this kind of mess. Not feeling like this.

I'm not a puker, and that's something to be proud of in certain circles, but there's always a price. On a scale of one to ten, this hangover is definitely an eight. I only reached ten once, and that was a near death experience in Mexico. Forgive me if I don't want to think about it right now. Alas, there is only one thing to be done: Clean as much as one can, then go back to bed. Do it in shifts this way until it's all better. Then, as dusk approaches, choke down a beer or something and kill the headache.

There are certain things that make cleaning up after a party invariably worse. Polaroids, for instance. Who needs to see these washed-out scenes of depravity mixed in with the carnage of bottles and ashtrays? There's a rule. If you stop to look at one of these snapshots the next morning, you will discover that you're standing in something sticky. Not spilled gin!

The one good thing about this apartment is I can open the curtains wide and no one can see the devastation. I'm too high up. Officially I'm on 24, but there's no 13th floor, so I guess it's 23. The reason they don't put 13th floors in these buildings is really just the distance from the ground. If you live below 13, you're still connected to life at ground level. Above this, people below start looking like ants. The noise from the street is diffused. The elevator ride becomes more like a commute. Anyone who's lived above 13 for more than a year would be a good candidate for space travel. You know what it's like to look down at the world with a kind of fondness for home that's always defeated by the effort it actually takes to go down there. Anyway, the people who make these buildings don't want you to dwell on it, so they leave out the important 13th floor.

Someone put gum on one of the cacti.

Asshole. I'll tidy that up when my hands stop shaking. And no hangover would be perfect without mitigating circumstances. For this one, someone has chosen to move in next door. No matter how discreet I try to be, I know that I'll end up in the elevator, reeking of booze, sweating, with two garbage bags full of cigarette ends and half-eaten canapés. Stuck with me for the ride will be my new neighbour, delighted at the wonderful impression of me, the guy next door.

I tried to lie down earlier, but the new tenant was pushing heavy furniture about on the other side of my bedroom wall. Maybe out of spite, I'll just stack the empties out in the hall before taking them down.

Oh god. You sit down for a second and the waves of thick, lethargic nausea pass by again. Memories surface of how the night ended: Someone's new girlfriend singing about a well-hung fisherman, and everyone's stupid laughter. . . . How the whale took the bait, I remember. Stumbling out, too loud in the hallway, though the neighbours next door are not easily offended. They're good people, but deviant, decadent alcoholics to a man, and they like my place for parties as it's the highest apartment of all. It's not a good way to be popular, but the best view comes with a kind of prestige.

You can open a window this high up and freshen the air in about ten seconds. And you can stare out, hoping to catch a glimpse of some other unlucky fool mopping up after a similar soirée. From here, I have seen some wonderful parties. The best are the rooftops in the summertime, when everyone hangs those idiotic chili lights. Once in a while you catch sight of revelers going too far, throwing up over balconies, or passing out and being abused by their chums.

The view can be amazing sometimes. The night the big storm hit the east coast, you could look out and see entire buildings, lit from within by the blue-white light of twenty televisions, all flickering simultaneously on the same news channel. And you can hardly ever look out the window without seeing someone trying to pee in private. Behind bushes and dumpsters, in alleys and car parks, behind buildings, or right in the middle of the street. You'd think the ground down there was urine-soaked. But I digress.

The person moving in next door has to be all right. The first thing he or she's done is to hook up the stereo. Jazz filters down the hall over the bumps and grunts of heavy lifting. I can't make out the music exactly – the walls here are pretty thick – but I think it's either late Billie or early Nina. Whatever. In the depraved haze of my hangover, I get curious and look out the fisheye peephole, trying to catch a glimpse of the new person. There's a couple of fairly big guys, possibly just movers, shifting a lot of cardboard boxes into the front room. One of the boxes says "Magazines" on it. It's got to be a woman or a fag. The jazz was a clue, but anyone who moves with magazines. . . .

I never knew the previous tenant very well. I think he was a school teacher or something. He lived there with a horrible little cat who I did meet. I've never known a more unpleasant, vicious cat. He called it Tipper because it would stalk compulsively around his apartment tipping things off tables and shelves. Plants, books, candles, drinks, anything. Often, if the cat was alone for a very long time, you could hear things crashing to the floor next door. Once, I reached down to pet it in the hallway, and it tore a gash that you can still see out of my hand.

Oh well, back to it. More Tylenol, more water. More tidying of debris. This really is the best part of the party. Parties are always finer in recollection. Phone calls are exchanged in the afternoon between sore guests, already reminiscing like going over old times. The worse the hangover, the more distant the party seems in your past. Or, the more you want to distance it from the present. Stories out-shine or out-shame each other. Memories of friends, different crowds you hung out with, the guy who always shows up as the first guest and the first guy to get drunk. . . . Photographs stack up. Glowing moments between all these different families of people. Fabulous outfits. Amazing dinners. Good friends.

4

#805 – 1461 Harwood Street

Bricks piled up into fortresses. Jerking robotic movements replace the unpredictable and imperfect sensuality of the hand-made. Walls built to enclose the spaces, and then to divide by partitions, and then subdivide by the need to reduce and economize. Lines drawn with the best of intentions, but without forethought or guidance. Now the right angle is the man at the switch. Binary codes bounce between on and off, but with abandon. And the seven sins have coddled this process.

– J.'s notebook

As J.'s worldly belongings were disbursed to charities, his body crackled and turned to ash in a professionally tended funeral pyre. I didn't know what I was going to do with his ashes, but I felt strongly that something appropriate would take shape as I sorted out his papers. I had dragged home several boxes of books, notes, and drawings, with the intention of distilling some kind of explanation out of them. With the proceeds from J.'s "estate" I bought a selection of very good single malts, which I kept near the boxes of his papers, always close at hand.

I kept thinking back to one childhood Christmas when I discovered a twelve-thousand-piece jigsaw puzzle in a local store. I begged and pleaded with my parents for it, but they knew instinctively that it was the wrong side of my personality to cultivate. When it didn't turn up under the tree that year, I was terribly disappointed, but I also developed a new respect for my folks when they explained their thinking to me. If I really wanted the puzzle, they told me, I could buy it with my own money later.

I looked at the boxes in my dining room, at the papers that had already begun to spill across the table. There were little stacks starting to pile up as I vainly tried to sort and resort the thousands of images and words. This was no ordinary two-dimensional puzzle, but I was literally watching it do the same thing to me, feeding my obsessions, taking me further into my own head and further still from reality.

With the tape seal cracked on only one of
the boxes, I sat there at the table, whisky in
one hand, smoke in the other, and studied the
lines and angles in J.'s drawings. It was like he
had executed a perfect rendering of a regular
apartment building in 3D, but had left out all
the content of the structure. The internal
space of the building was indicated, but like a
ghost, there was no matter to fill its the volume. J.'s lines were thin and even, and perfectly straight, as though drawn with the help
of a computer, but they left the impression of
having been recorded by a sick man rather
than a master draughtsman.

There were stacks of these drawings,
maybe hundreds of them, sometimes showing
the same building from five or six different
angles. Little titles, written in the manner of
blueprints, were listed at the bottom of the
pages: "The Banffshire, 610 Jervis Street.
(1911)," or "Kensington Place, 1386 Nicola
Street. (1912)." They all seemed to be residential buildings in the West End, and some of
them were built in the eighties and nineties,
too. I wondered why he had bothered includ-
ing the dates they were built, as the drawings
seemed so specific to place, and identical in
style whether old or new.

There was an entire file of drawings and notes on The Capri at 1080 Barclay Street. Drawings made from the front and back of the building, from the sides, from down the block. . . . I wondered if he had actually sat on the street and sketched the building, but certain angles would have to be studies from impossible points of view, like from beneath street level, and from inside other buildings. A page of notes was attached:

> *The Capri is so even, so flat. Windows lined in parallel strips preclude balconies. Comfortable from any angle but facing the entrance: the giant box hangs uneasily off of its hill foundations, resting its bulk on four or five round pilotis, crushing the entrance and foyer beneath. The stairwell is exposed like a dorsal wound, the vertebrae of the structure visible from the street.*

And there was a newspaper clipping with no source or date, that told of a tenant in the corner apartment on the ground floor, facing Thurlow Street. It seems he had moved into the place after the previous tenant was evicted for offering sexual favours to passers-by on the sidewalk. She would simply open her window, and they'd climb through. The new tenant had been repeatedly disturbed by clients of the former renter, knocking at his window in the middle of the night. What was the connection? Why include this bizarre news story?

All of these observations and concerns that interested J. so much were external. There was no indication that he had ever entered the building, and no information on anything current or living about the place. Why would he have cared?

I gave up and began packing cleaners and rags into my bag. I still had to do the final tidying of J.'s empty apartment. It was the last obligation I had promised to his old landlady. Confusing thoughts filled my mind as I walked down to his apartment block. I could only think of the building as Bay Towers now. I approached its west-facing entrance and looked up, counting the ten floors. The frosted windows of apartment bathrooms, some lit, fell vertically with a kind of porthole effect down its side.

Approaching his eighth-floor door, I paused, the thought of knocking on his door quickly passing. I switched on the hallway light as I entered, and the stark whiteness of the walls took me by surprise. It was hard to imagine this apartment now containing anything of J.'s, let alone his life and work. The bare walls and floor crated a hollow, echoing effect as I walked from room to room. I realized that my task was to erase the last evidence of J.'s life here, as I opened all the blinds and windows to let some breathable air in.

The light fixture, hanging in what was J.'s dining room, looked strange without a roomful of objects to illuminate, and it cast yellow light and abstract shadows onto the walls. The space felt emptier than it was, like a container rather than a home. The light fixtures, woodwork, electrical sockets, and phone jacks took on a profoundly utilitarian look, and somewhere deep inside my mind, a kind of anxiety swelled. I shook myself as though from a dream.

Bleach lay in little pools, cutting through the greasy residue behind the fridge and under the stove. Pine-scented disinfectant dried on the mopped floors of the bedrooms and hallway. The citrus smell of window cleaner dispersed rapidly into the rooms. While all of these chemicals were reacting and polishing, my mind must have been completely blank, as the time passed quickly, and the job was nearly done.

I stood back, admiring my work, and smoked a cigarette out the window. Tapping some ashes, I looked directly down and wondered why J. hadn't merely jumped from here. Eighty feet below was the concrete entrance to the parking lot, and it occurred to me that J.'s purposes would have been better served by having this pad of concrete stop his falling body with an exhibitionistic thump. But that was it – J.'s condition was not for show.

I looked at the space that the couch J. had died on had occupied. The volume of space taken up by his dead body hung there, now empty and unmarked. The next tenant would maybe watch television from that spot, maybe have sex. Or perhaps that void would never be filled again, protect itself and remain empty and sacred until the building was demolished years later. I had approached and passed my hand through the empty space before I realized what I was doing. For some reason, it scared me, so I busied myself, packing up the solvents and brushes.

I returned the key to the landlady, and she stood there watching me as I waited for the elevator. I tried to read her expression, but her calm smile must have been in a foreign language as it registered nothing that I could identify. She thanked me and said, "Bye-bye," in a little voice as though she were speaking to some young child. The entire end of the evening had been disturbing somehow, and I was delighted to be free, and back on the street heading home.

5

#502 – 610 Jervis Street

I must move from here. Is the apartment itself making me think like this? Something hidden in the structure of this place torments me day and night, and I am beginning to think this whole block of flats was constructed with the intention of driving me mad. Perhaps a reasoned approach will help. History, background. That seems to be the root of the problem at any rate.

Who could work in an archive without falling into the spiraling obsession of history? I have been the clerk there for too long, I fear. Every researcher, each historian and genealogist tempts me with the forbidden pleasure of discovery. I have seen it in their eyes, the elation of making that final connection, the trauma of the missing link to the story. They come to make sense, I think, by locating themselves in time and place, and building a world around them. One chap used to come here driven by some anxiety that buildings caused for him. Apparently, the placement of buildings and their relative heights drove him to distraction. He would try to explain it to me, desperate to be understood, but how can these things be explained?

It was easy for me to fall prey to the search for meaning. Three generations of my family have lived here. Before that, they arrived en masse from the UK, and even then, the family history is all recorded, sitting like a goldmine of madness, just waiting to be plundered. And my family history is a special case, or so it seems. Obviously someone from a previous generation found it equally compelling, as the records are very thorough. Perhaps it is all a trap, laid down by some sadistic ancestor in a complex practical joke. Shall I start at the beginning or the end?

My paternal great-grandfather was a high level freemason, respected in his community. His bizarre death was big news, and the clippings still exist at the archives. He was something of a success story in my family, reaching a far greater age than anyone else. But as he approached ninety, his mind began to go and he developed autolalia, a kind of manic chattering, continuous talking. He would have driven anyone around him mad with his incessant, nonsensical banter. Perhaps his nurse strangled him in frustration, but she reported that he actually talked himself to death, eventually choking on his own words.

His two sons, wealthy as they were, moved here to escape the fate of their family, I think. One became a popular city councilor, while the other, my grandfather, became an architect. One day my grandfather's brother was taking a walk in the park, apparently across an open field, when he was struck by a huge, falling tree. No explanation can be found for how he was crushed beneath a tree in the middle of a field. My grandfather outlived him by several years, but joined him in time. He became tipsy at a celebration in honour of his building designs, and somehow drowned in the garden pond of the Lieutenant Governor's mansion.

The family of my second cousins all fell prey to this mysterious inclination for bizarre deaths. One of them fell down a historic well while on tour of India. Another was mauled, allegedly by frantic seabirds on a fishing trip. My great aunt died in labour, producing Siamese twins who perished soon after. Her sister was a nun in the service of local chari- ties, but was institutionalized for her obsession

with embroidery. Her compulsion to embroi-
der with finer and finer detail drove her mad.

My own father stumbled on the street and
was dragged right across town, stuck in the
undercarriage of a trolley bus. His sister over-
dosed on narcotics that she took to allay the
fears of her impending death. Her one son,
my only first cousin, was found dead in
Rangoon, his body containing the venom of
four different deadly snakes.

It goes back further in time, too. Ancestors
burned at the stake, cannibalized during a
famine, crushed during the construction of
the parish church. What possible way can I
live with this knowledge? My entire family
has handed down a genetic trait for unusual
and accidental deaths. If nothing else, my fate
was sealed the moment I took the position at
the archives, with all the information hiding
there in the books and records. A trap waiting
to be sprung.

Perhaps the most terrifying notion, the
most bizarre coincidence of all, was my discovery that I currently live in a building
designed by my own grandfather. Did he play
a role in this? Before stumbling drunk into a
decorative pond, did he leave some trap for
me in this place? I stare at the walls here,

uncertain about their structural integrity. How much weight can the floors of this building actually sustain before caving in, flushing me and all my possessions onto the streets below? I lie awake at night, thinking about the concrete pad beneath my bed, beneath my floor, dangling there, in space. I dream of vertigo. How can I actually move from here, when the simple act of taking the elevator or stairwell fills me with terror?

So here I am, trapped both by time and place. Stuck here to passively follow in the traditions of my genealogy. It may be that my search for meaning in my life was the mistake I made, the quest for the forbidden fruit of understanding. Or perhaps the revelations that were made in archives and libraries and family trees were fatefully laid out, waiting for me to uncover. Either way, I have actually reached a point of paranoia or something close, where coincidence is no longer amusing. Everything points in the same direction, and I am afraid.

6

#318 – 1235 Nelson Street

We are the agents of the right angle in a universe that thrives in its absence. Filers, data technicians, and taxonomers are the new artists, looking to the future, moving the project forward. Architects, economists, and city planners have hidden the progression of the right angle from us, encouraging us, forcing us to live within its bounds. Now that we are here, most of us are in denial: We can't have lost.

– J.'s notebook

In the dark, you are there, watching me sleep. For a moment I pretend I'm still asleep, and then sit up in the bed, relieved to not have to play dead for you. You come closer and I reach out to touch. My hand passes through you; your solid form, the volume of you, passes around and through my fingers. Your body fades in detail, leaving only your outer dimensions formed somehow by the light itself.

This is what I woke up to. Dreams obsessing on the once-occupied space of J.'s body. I get up and head to the bathroom and just down the hall is the dining room table strewn now with J.'s neuroses. His fucking ashes are still there, days later, in the bizarre paint can box the crematorium handed over. The space his body occupies now is a paperweight, still holding down the files and pictures that I thought offered an insight into his madness.

The whole thing seems ridiculous. I have friends. I have normal, day-to-day things to do. The thought of not having left my apartment for two days makes me worry. I don't want to go where J. went.

I made coffee and lit a cigarette, sitting away from the table to avoid visual contact with the maelstrom of J.'s insides. His paint can. I made plans to go out, unaffected, and visit friends, walk in the park, hang out on the seawall. Feeling the hit of the coffee, I got dressed and packed some paper and a pen into my pocket in case I chose to record my thoughts outside the apartment. It felt like a prescription, but I ignored it like I ignored the dining room table.

I left the flat, and was not down more than

one of the three flights of stairs when I remembered a map I had seen in J.'s papers. It showed various routes of his walks through the West End, and it suddenly became important that I hadn't made specific plans for my outing. I caught myself. "Crazy," I said aloud, and noticed it as I continued down the steps.

I stopped outside my building in the light rain. Against something I realized was my better judgment, I looked back at the building for a moment, and saw only 1235 Nelson Street. For just a second there was only the building instead of home. Three rows of art deco eyes: windows staring out around a lionesque nose into the street. I thought how absolutely fucked this was, not because I had noticed the menacing face of my building for the first time, but rather that I had turned around at all. I had to look back as though to make sure J's crap-heap wasn't following me or something.

I returned to my apartment.

The books which J. filled, his journals and what-not, went on for volumes. Notes on buildings in the West End of Vancouver. It was all notes. Try going out on the street and really noticing the buildings around you and when you get home, write enough about your findings

to fill a page. It isn't easy. J. had recorded
everything. Floors, windows, balconies, doors:

*1655 Barclay – It is a triumph of Soviet
and Thatcherite design. It is not so much
an apartment block as a great wall. Windows punched into the concrete with the
certainty of machines and great vertical
expanses of long balconies, bedecked in the
summer with plants like a water fall of
greenery. The flatness of the front façade
is awe inspiring. Surely this model succeeds
where the others fail to inspire. Passing
this, I can only despise the anticlimax of
lowrise condominiums in their tree-lined
abundance. Whole blocks of wasteful
angular brown and grey condos. The pro-
tected courtyards, behind their locked sec-
urity fences, fill me with loneliness and
despair. Each one should be bulldozed to
make room for more truly elegant and
more economical architecture.*

*God's final gift to mankind after the
circle was the right angle. Engorged, effi-
cient, the rectangle is truly perfect. Look
at Lord Stanley Tower and behold the
mystery of the rectangle. Its facets glisten,
even in the rain.*

Nuts. Nuts! I tried to separate myself from the alien logic in front of me. Surely I would drown in this. I found one of the maps, a kind of suggested walking tour of the West End, and rushed to the sidewalk. I needed to get out.

I intercepted one of J.'s walking routes where Jervis and Nelson Streets meet, and continued up Nelson, turning left onto Nicola two blocks up. The rain was getting heavier, and I walked quickly. I was beginning to notice details of structure and topography that I had never thought about before in this place where I had lived for the last ten years. The way the whole area slopes down into English Bay, and the actual steepness of the hill on various streets. I turned left on Comox Street, right on Cardero, left again on Pendrell. I noticed the kids leaving Lord Roberts School in little groups, and wondered what time I actually left my apartment if it was already after three.

I seemed to be the only one on the street without an umbrella, and I could feel the rain beneath my clothes. I became self-conscious for a couple of blocks, imagining my wet, white skin and crazed eyes, my manic pace. I must have looked like quite the freak. I wanted to return home where it was safe and dry. Looking up in any direction I could see the moss and vines clinging to the wet shells of buildings, warm yellow light issuing from windows. Was this agoraphobia? Did J. know how this felt?

I continued down the hill on Bidwell, where it meets Beach, and took shelter from the rain in the gazebo in Alexandra Park. The wind off the water was cold and bracing, and I huddled there, wondering what I was doing. Gazing over the hundreds of carved initials and meaningless graffiti in the bandstand, I thought of my own friends, how I had vanished from our little scene. Any one of them would commit me if they found me here. I promised myself I would phone someone when I got home, set up a meeting at the bar, confess my mad sins, but I wasn't about to go there now, not in this state.

They were going to put a giant AIDS memorial here once, in this little park, but the homophobes of the West End pooh-poohed the idea. I couldn't help feeling bitter. I wondered why J.'s death, out of all the people I knew who had died, had such a firm hold on my psyche. None of this was sad. I had not mourned the loss of J., as I hardly knew him, but it was more than that. There was no compelling reason for me to care about his suicide except as one of those things you mention over drinks. "Huh," friends would say noncommitally. "Too bad. I wonder how he did it."

I chose a different route home, but avoided Harwood and Nicola where some stranger had probably already moved into J.'s old suite. As I walked up the hill something hit me like a flash of light: the top floor of a twenty-storey block of apartments on Beach Avenue was probably at the exact same altitude as my third-floor apartment on Nelson. Could that be? The notion appealed to me, but with a kind of vague anxiety. It was completely meaningless to my rational mind, but something floated there, some new understanding, like evidence of J.'s fixations.

Suddenly I was inside my own apartment, taking off my wet clothes and shoes. I had just appeared there, like the walk home hadn't happened. It didn't matter. Chunks of time disappearing from my life were the least of my concerns. I hurried into the bathroom to dry my hair, and settled quickly at the dining room table, sifting my hands through the stacks of J.'s clues with a new urgency. It was beginning to make sense. I had been looking for meaning all this time, and I had only just considered that there was no meaning. There were no perceptible connections here, and I wasn't going crazy. Pieces were falling into place just beyond my intellect, and it was exciting, compelling, and new.

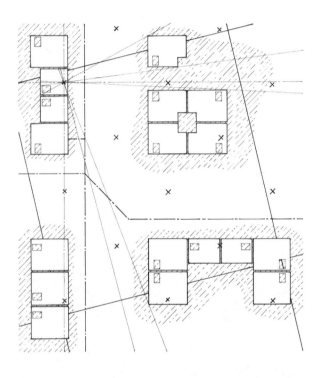

7

#2402 – 1808 Comox Street

This is the thirteenth building he has lived in downtown. The apartments have been so similar in cases that he has to sit down with pen and paper to actually tell you where he's lived. The whole process of moving, of saying goodbye, is utterly familiar to him. This time, however, he is sad. He knows that transitions often go well together, so when he broke up with his boyfriend, he decided, what the hell, *he* might as well move, too.

The movers have left, and he thanks the stars that he took his friends' advice to hire them rather than lugging all his stuff by himself. Opening a beer, he moves a box off his chair and sits. Here is his entire life, everything he owns, in cartons, bags, and suitcases, the furniture in various states of assembly. He gets into that mood that he always gets at this point, though a little sadder this time, back amongst the single bachelors again. He always thinks about how he could sell all the books and furniture, the orchids, the stereo, the entire lot. He could take a trip, move somewhere warm for a year or two. Go and see his brother. But he never does.

This new space he's living in, for however long, still feels impersonal, desolate somehow. Even when his shelves are up, the posters hung, the stereo filling his home with his own music, even then it will take a while before he will feel at ease here. As used as he is to the pressures and emotions of moving, he still doesn't feel like he's had a real home for many years. He catches himself, and makes himself busy, tidying, arranging, organizing, putting things away. Everything he owns has its place, and finding it is something he can do with his eyes closed. The television will go over there, beside it, the tall lamp. Knives go on the left, then forks, teaspoons, and tablespoons on the right. There is a correct sequence for him as he moves things to and fro.

Billie Holiday on the stereo. Is he trying to depress himself even more?

The apartment has a wonderful view, but everything's too fresh. He cannot enjoy the view without thinking of his ex, and how fevered he would become with all these new views into people's lives. His ex is a colossal pervert, fetishistic about nearly everything, but particularly about watching other people. The old voyeur would really enjoy this space. You can see everyone in town.

He pulls himself together. His ex couldn't even recall how long they'd been together, let alone their anniversary. These details meant nothing to him, for he was so caught up in his own psyche. They never really understood each other. They got together because they looked good that way, and they had fun. But for both of them, the things that mattered to the other were miles away from reality.

He remembers going home for the first time with this guy. He seemed really bright, well mannered, eloquent.... His place was full of novels by some really good writers, and it made an impression. Then he learned that not one of these books had actually been read. Each one was carefully chosen because as a younger man, their owner spent much time masturbating over the author photographs of middle-aged women. Wow. Dorris Lessing, Angela Carter, Maeve Binchy, Iris Murdoch, Anne Tyler, even Simone de Beauvoir and

Margaret Laurence. "Everyone but Atwood," he used to say.

That was the first sign he should have taken seriously. Stop thinking about it.

Just passing certain buildings on the sidewalk brings back memories with astounding clarity. Doorways and buzzer codes, the idiosyncrasies of an elevator. Glancing up from a passing car window, he can suddenly remember conversations, misadventures, certain smells. . . . They represent pieces, chapters of his life, episodes involving different lovers, angry landlords – remember that place with the silverfish? He notices how nostalgic he is being and tries to dwell on something else, but always without forgetting.

The person or people who live next door in this building show all the signs of being the wild party type. Paper grocery bags filled with empty liquor bottles stand outside the door. He is curious, maybe worried. He wonders if his ex has ever spent a depraved evening behind that door, cheating with someone who would be willing to participate more fully. For a moment he hates his new neighbour, but it passes. He imagines a sexual god in there, just behind the wall, traipsing about in his nude glory.

There is a smell of litter boxes in the bathroom, so he unpacks all his fragrant soaps and colognes first. The curtains in the bedroom are tattered at the bottom, quite obviously by a cat. With about ten projects half done already, he begins taking the curtains down, out of their little hooks, and makes plans to buy horizontal blinds. This is the way he has amassed most of his possessions, slowly improving each space he has lived in, then carting it all to the next place. He never paints an apartment, and now he even avoids putting nails in the walls for fear of losing his deposit. He is an expert.

In a week, mail will begin to appear in his box with the familiar yellow change-of-address stickers covering his name. The cable company will make excuses as to why their worker can't possibly connect him up for a fortnight. He expects to discover that at least one of the burners on his stove needs mending, and that the freezer ices up if you open the refrigerator more than once a day. The toilet will stick in refill mode so he'll have to jiggle the handle. In one building, the radiator was so loud, he became convinced that someone in another apartment was striking theirs with a hammer. Oh yes, he's an expert.

He looks out at the cold grey sky and wonders what the sunsets will be like from here. He is so tied to where he has come from, but he is also free. His priorities have changed once more, and he awaits the filling in of his new life with all its complicated details. He knows his ex just isn't the sort to mourn a breakup. He'd probably just have a party. But this is neither here nor there right now. Of course it is. The CD comes to an end, and Billie's digitalized voice has said her piece. As time goes by.

8

1160 Davie Street
Byron's Lounge

The brilliance of the side meeting the corner, the box inside the box. . . . It's all such utter genius! I have tried for so long to reproduce in draughting the perfection of the right angle, and I think now that it cannot be done. The right angle insinuates itself, it is not produced. Instead of marveling at it, we embrace it blindly, and only later discover that we cannot survive within it. The single, unique enemy of the right angle is love. And now I love the right angle.

– J.'s notebook

I was half-way out the door again. Sitting there at the table, and really meaning to be on my way down to the Parkhill Hotel on Davie Street. I had my shoes on, and took some consolation in that, but the boxes of images and words saved from J.'s apartment walls sat beckoning me. It felt like I could enter each

building in the West End, every single apartment, to the top floors of the very newest
condo towers, and none of these would supply
me with as good a view as the things in these
boxes. The missing patterns in all of J.'s mad
wallpaper had begun to settle into place, coat-
ing the insides of my skull.

The problem I faced was not just how J.
had chosen to tape all these pieces into place,
but why he chose different rooms, why some
things were covered up, and others, fresher in
meaning somehow. And there was an addi-
tional, more basic mystery of why he chose
them in the first place.

Postcard: a young, apparently Chinese
child, probably a girl, but only three years old
maybe, stands in a courtyard amongst clay
buildings, casually holding on to the tail of a
very large pig. The pig must have been eight
or nine times the weight of the child. It is
completely oblivious to the child and whoever
took the photo. Head down in a trough, it
ignores the entire scene. A surreal joke of a
postcard with no discernible punchline.

Postcard: DeNiro as Travis Bickle from *Taxi
Driver*, head shaved to a mohawk, two huge
pistols held aloft, and that menacing, devious
grin of a total madman. I got up and went to

my bookshelves, checking my own copy of Paul Schrader's screenplay. This scene is called "The Slaughter," and the same still is reprinted. No clue.

Postcard: a detail from Fra Angelico's *Annunciation*, showing the angel Gabriel announcing to Mary that she's pregnant with the child of God. Again, I consulted my books. It's from the first chapter of Luke, verses 26–38. I considered hauling out my copy of the Bible, but paused, instead looking at the perfectly vaulted ceiling of Mary's little chamber in the painting, its parabolic arches and classical columns....

News clipping: a story on newsprint, browned by age, of the Canada goose population in Stanley Park, and how they have caused consistent problems for traffic heading towards the Lions Gate Bridge. The language is light, and meant to be amusing, but relays the image of enraged drivers, impatient and already late for work.

On and on like this, hundreds, thousands of seemingly unrelated images and data. I pulled out a black-and-white postcard of Patti LaBelle taken in the seventies. She looks great, full of life. I found a roll of masking tape in a kitchen drawer and affixed the image to the wall above the table. I circled the table, looking at her from different angles. She looked good up there on the wall. Humming along with only a few of the actual lyrics, I put on my coat to "Lady Marmalade," the only LaBelle song I could think of, and almost surprised myself by just getting up and leaving.

They were waiting for me at the Lounge. Three friends that only ever left the corner table to work and sleep. The rest of the time, at least one of them was always there, sipping the pale ale and getting poetic. Our little corner of the Lounge was totally out of place amongst the hotel guests who sat at the bar, but we had been going so regularly and for so long that it didn't matter any more. I could have been found here, often by myself, right up until J. entered my life with such force. I missed the place, and I missed my friends, and the cushioned bench felt good and natural as I joined them.

Silence.

"Where have you been?"

I smiled. "Man, I don't even know."

"What's up?"

"I'm still working on J.'s stuff."

They looked at each other. I could guess the meaning of this. I had been "working on

J.'s stuff" for an unacceptably long time. Speculations had obviously been made between them. This wasn't the sort of thing to make me feel wary, but just that I needed to catch up and so did they.

"I know. . . . I've been working on it for too long."

"I didn't say that." And she hadn't.

"I'm just finding it all quite interesting. J. made these drawings which are quite spectacular, real thin lines, and accurate, too."

"I didn't know he was an artist."

More glances.

"What?" I wanted them to just get to the point.

My beer arrived, and as I took my first sip, one of them got up to visit the loo, and another changed the subject.

"I'm writing a novel."

"How's it going?" I asked without caring, suddenly having second thoughts about this whole meeting. I wanted to return to the stacks of postcards.

"It's going all right. I want it to make me the darling of Canadian fiction."

Laughs all around. This was easier. Things were coming back to normal. I ended up staying for a few more pints, strangely glad to find myself relaxing again, with the knowledge that J.'s stuff was safe at my place, ready for me to begin again at my leisure. They complained about work, about freaky customers and unsound management decisions. They psychoanalyzed various couples we knew.

One of them had to leave, and then another. Both said little parting lines like they cared without wanting to know what I was up to. "Well, I hope we'll see more of you before too long.... You look good." This was a lie. I knew I looked like shit. I felt gaunt, straggly, disheveled.

The two of us sat there waiting for something to happen, to break the ice, or something. It seemed odd that in this little group of friends, we all knew each other so well, and for so long, but we continually faced these awkward moments of caring too much about each other's crises. One of us was always splitting up, falling in love, trying too hard or not hard enough at whatever. Of all the people in the world, this was my true family. I felt like I could tell them anything in principle, but reality was always just a thing that coexisted with us, and rarely allowed for genuine honesty.

The waitress we all knew by name replenished our pints and freshened the ashtray.

"Long time no see," she said, addressing me with reserved care.

"Yeah, I know."

She left us alone, and then the question arose. "So what's really going on?" She took another sip and pushed the ashtray towards me.

"I think I'm slipping...." I heard myself confess it, and didn't feel any better for doing so. "There's something wrong with J.'s stuff. It's like there's a puzzle that I just can't put together. I was only supposed to lock up after his apartment was cleaned out, but I can't stop there."

"Do you think he was nuts?"

"Yes. No! He wasn't nuts. I don't know." I wasn't sure at that point that I could deal with one of her interrogations. She's always giving this very good, very sound advice that takes you down the path of most resistance. She won't stand for easy answers, and conversations in the past that have started quite innocently have ended in tears. I couldn't lie to her.

"I don't think he was crazy, but he had a totally different way of seeing things, and I guess I'm just trying to figure out what was different. In one way his life made complete sense, all ordered and everything, but he was also totally obsessed, and he killed himself, for chrissake." The tin was open and the beans were spilling out.

"What was he obsessed about?"

"Buildings. Or architecture. I don't know. I think he wanted to understand something about the nature of residential apartment blocks. . . . That does sound crazy." I paused. "But it kind of makes sense to me, and I don't know how."

"Did you get his ashes?"

"They're on my dining room table right now." Once more, as I was saying things, I could hear the insanity of it all. Why hadn't I dumped his ashes? How could I be living with the burned-up corpse of someone I hardly knew in my own home?

"What are you going to do?"

"With what, the ashes?"

"No, what are you going to do with yourself? Isn't it time you gave this a rest?"

Then it just clicked. Here I was, trying to confide, to seek advice, to be rescued by the people I relied on for rescue situations, and they all just thought I was losing it. The explanation ended there. J. had nothing to do with this.

"You don't know! J. understood stuff. He had made sense of things. He killed himself because his project was complete."

"Oh, right, so you're trying to figure out his little secret, and when you're crazy enough too, you'll kill yourself as well?"

"I'm not going to kill anyone."

I walked home in the rain that had started again. I wasn't happy. I didn't feel like the feedback my friends had offered was of any use. They didn't understand. You can't rely on friends. It felt good to see them and everything, but it was just a window outside of myself, and I felt worse for it somehow. I felt like I had betrayed J.'s trust.

I was angry, and lines from the conversation kept turning over in my mind. "Look!" I wanted to say, "Can't you see? Are you all blind?!" By the time I got home I was in a foul mood. I stormed into my apartment and walked straight over to the table. I took the Flutoxocet out of one of the boxes. J. was not crazy!

Postcards: a roomful of women in the 1920s, all dressed as men. False moustaches, pipes, bowler hats, each one with a suit and tie. Six children dressed as cats for a play or something, bows around their necks, smiling, tails tucked uniformly around their sides. The Man Ray photograph of an extreme close-up of a woman's face, lashes thick with mascara, and cheeks dotted with glass beads to simulate tears. Two men at a table, one is Houdini I think, and beneath the table he holds a large bell in his toes. They are surrounded by other men, possibly elected officials, or the clergy, watching skeptically.

9

#805 - 1461 Harwood Street

You're going to love this place: one thousand square feet, hardwood floors, two bedrooms (that's one for us, and one for my office), great view.... They just repainted in here, and half my stuff hasn't arrived yet, so it looks really empty. I'll have to get a phone jack put into the office area, but other than that, it's perfect. Mother would even approve. With the money we save on the rent, we'll be able to afford a house after the first year, and, you know, maybe by then we will need more space for a baby.

And my new position is going great, too. I've never had such a smooth transfer. The company is going to pay for everything. They're also going to pay for my gas when I'm travelling, but don't worry, I won't be away too much. Most of it I can do from here, because we've got such a good electronic promotions package. Flutoxocet never looked better!

I've met some of the reps for other products, and they're all really nice. We've got a great team by the looks of things, and we're going to kick butt. You'll really like Andrew and his wife Claire, but she's a bit uptight. They've got a little girl already. I think they named her Courtney, so we'll have to think of something else if it's a girl. They're already talking about having another baby. We'll have dinner with them when you get here, and you'll see what I mean. They're great.

Andrew and I went skiing last weekend, and Claire said she'd come by and water the plants and pick up the newspaper, so I gave her the keys. When we got back she was all upset about something to do with the apartment. She said she didn't like the place, which was a bit rude. I don't know what she was talking about. Andrew said she gets depressed sometimes. Whatever! I'm going to refer them to Bob, my therapist. She can't go around talking about ghosts for too long, or she's going to get locked up. Anyway, she's really nice aside from that, and he's a good buddy to have. They're dying to meet you, and I can't wait to show off my beautiful little wife. I miss you.

Next week there's a big motivational seminar at the company that sounds kind of exciting.

Andrew tripled sales in his product category, so he's going to give a talk or something. I hope I can do that, too, and he says he'll show me the ropes. Walter, our department head, drinks too much, and Andrew says we can really get away with anything because he's usually asleep when he does show up for work. Walter's a good guy, aside from his drinking, but we do all the work and he takes all the credit.

Mother was complaining about all the gays who live down here, but you hardly ever notice them, and some of them are really nice. I guess she's just old-fashioned. She still calls them faggots, and she's got to stop. If she found out about your brother, and how I met you, she'd die, so I suppose we'll just have to live with that secret. I know you have a hard time with her, but she really likes you. You two will come around.

Anyway, I can't wait to show you. The seawall is right here, there's a gym just down the street, and there's some great restaurants. It's a super neighbourhood, really safe, and you can just feel that this apartment has good karma. You can catch a little ferry over to the island market, and they even rent kayaks down there, so who knows? If we learn how to do it, we can go out with Andrew and Claire.

Oh well, I should get back to work now. E-mail me back when you get this.

Love you. Kiss kiss.

Chad.

Oh! I almost forgot! I talked to the landlady, and she says we can't have a cat, so you'll have to leave Ginger there. See you soon!

10

#318 - 1235 Nelson Street

The curving notions of God and creation, heaven and hell, are excellent excuses, but they don't make sense. The right angle excludes nonsense. Even when people fully realize the wonder of ninety degrees, as in pyramid building cultures and skyscraper construction, they fail to appreciate that it is something outside of humanity. With all the logical and chaotic perfection of the natural world simplified, the right angle triumphs. Only by reaching a profound understanding of, a passionate connection to the right angle can we defeat it.

– J.'s notebook

I cracked the seal on the J.'s reserve Flutoxocet supply. The little blue pill went down easily with a strange, chemical taste that I washed away with a swig of scotch. I paused, waiting like I always did after swallowing a drug, as if the effects would be felt immediately. Nothing.

My conversation at the Lounge with my supposed friends was still racing through my mind. Did I want someone to have saved me?

I had begun clipping news items from the local papers, perhaps to give J.'s work a chronological continuity into my own life. One story in particular seemed highly significant to the project, and actually got me started. It concerned an employee of the city archives who had been killed outright when his building's wrought-iron fire escape had collapsed around him. Apparently the entire structure had simply fallen away from the building, an incident that shocked the other tenants, and caused much concern for the local fire authorities. No mention was made about whether the victim had been on or merely beneath the falling iron work. I wondered if J. had known the man.

I snatched one of the volumes of J.'s writing from the table and flipped to a random page. He was describing the development of what seemed to be a kind of horizontal vertigo. A dizzying trepidation about the ground's right-angled relationship to the vertical side of a building. There was a quote from *Invisible Cities* by Italo Calvino: "The traveller recognizes the little that is his, discovering the much he has not had and will never have."

I puzzled on this for a moment. Out of the context of the book, which I still hadn't read, the quote was mysterious. Did J. consider himself a traveller? Or, like me, could he see himself going insane? I had been noticing new behaviours and new sentiments in myself for too long not to think my own fall was obvious. One doesn't notice that one is insane until just after doing something wildly irrational. One can sit back and say, "My God, that thing I just did was totally insane!" But you don't see it happening. You wonder still, at what precise moment does an individual cease to be who he thinks he is?

Even if I had come to understand what there was to be understood in J.'s sensibilities, the question still arose as to why he actually went that extra step and took his own life. I had to assume that the process of developing this new understanding of architecture was the same for J. as it was for me, but I was not plagued by urges to kill myself. I felt strangely incomplete about this, as though I had missed an important step in my studies. If I was not yet suicidal, I was missing something good. I continued reading.

J. talked about the folded nature of apart-ment layouts, how in order to maximize the economy of the space, there was always a room behind every wall. Some of them were in one apartment, some in another. Every hallway, each closet, hides another space altogether. The inner side of a building's outer walls were especially significant. They seemed the same, and felt the same as the wall behind which you knew another person's apartment lay, but to pass through them would mean to fall to your death. I imagined J. hunched over, listening with a glass held against the exterior walls of his building, straining to eavesdrop on neighbours that he knew weren't there.

The pill was doing something to me. It wasn't so much visual as linear. Something about the view of the lines in my flat had changed, like I was looking at them through a video camera rather than my own eyes. It was fascinating. Moving my head to pan my eyes over the room, my brain was interpreting this as the room moving around my head. I stood up from the table and felt a bit dizzy. The floor looked a lot farther away from me now, although I could see my feet down there. Trippy! I wondered what buildings would look like during a drug haze like this, but I was far too apprehensive to actually go outside.

People were looking into my flat through the windows. I could feel the icy stares, so I closed all the curtains and dimmed the lighting. My head was reeling. I looked at the piles of J's things strewn about my table, and they suddenly appeared in extreme close-up.

I must have been unconscious for some time. I woke up laying beside my bed, face down, naked. Somewhere in the apartment, a tiny noise, a faint hum was issuing forth, like a wrist watch alarm deep in someone's pocket. I sat on the bed, clutching my head like it might explode. My brain throbbed with the little buzzing noise, like it was full of bees trying to escape. I managed to put on a kimono and had to support myself against the doorway as I peered into the dining room. My heart sank.

The wall space above the table was covered in pictures and drawings. J's stuff had begun to migrate up the surface of the wall like a wave of insane ideas crashing into the shore. Shreds of masking tape were everywhere. I walked into the room, astonished, struggling to remember the end of the evening. I had absolutely no memory of sticking the pictures up there, but likewise, how I ended up beside my bed and not in it was missing, too. I looked about at the clutter, and the papers still stacked on the table. The buzzing noise was louder now, coming from the table itself, or. . . .

When I realized that it was J.'s ashes that were humming, I grabbed the can, shaking the contents to stop it. It continued buzzing as I packed the can into my satchel, and rushed to the kitchen cupboards in search of more scotch. I shoved the half-empty bottle into the bag and returned to my bedroom to dress in haste. J. was letting me know it was time to distribute his ashes, to repack his belongings, to store them away for a long time and be done with all this. *Buzz buzz buzz*. I searched madly for my keys, and grabbed the bag, heavy with J's remains, and headed for the door, shoving the bottle of Flutoxocet down into my coat pocket.

I startled a neighbour as I slammed my apartment door and headed for the street. She muttered something out of concern for me, but I ignored her and ran down the stairs. I didn't know where I was heading, but it felt urgent that I disperse J.'s ashes. It felt like I had one last window of opportunity to do this, or it would never happen. He would let me know where to dump them. The buzzing grew louder as I ran across the marble floor of the foyer and towards the front door.

11

#1005 - 1498 Harwood Street

We love to watch. The best thing about apartment living is the watching. Neither of us can remember where we first heard it, but there are two kinds of people in the West End: those with their blinds and curtains always open – the exhibitionists – and those with the windows always covered – the voyeurs. Well, it's true to a point, but the lines sometimes blur. We love to watch, but it's even better when they know you're watching.

There's a guy who lived across from us and one down. Cute. One of us would lie on the floor with the binoculars, while the other would give a massage. He knew we were looking. We learned about all there was to his life this way, just watching. He had a really set schedule of routines. Back from work, he would pour a beer or whiskey (he was always drinking) and sit at a table right in front of the window. We think he was an architect or something, because he was always drawing buildings and looking at maps. We love cute guys.

We weren't really interested in him until we noticed him watching us back. We would dare each other to walk about in the nude or do bizarre things for his benefit. He would sit there, trying to figure us out. Once in a while, the three of us would be watching each other, all very obvious. This became a really strange relationship for a while, with us sometimes even fucking while he looked on. He became accustomed to us seeing him nude, but he never brought anyone home, so we didn't even know if he was gay – you know, was he getting turned on by this like we were? It was hard to tell. Once in a while he would hold up one of his building sketches for our approval and we'd always hold up some centrefold from a skin magazine. At least he would laugh. We love laughter.

We don't get vertigo. Both of us could spend our whole lives just hanging out up here and watching them down there, though it would be better if we were higher up in the building. A better view, and less chance of somebody complaining. Our humble little life would provide some interesting views for onlookers, and there's a lot of seniors in these buildings. We don't want to offend anyone. Neither of us remember a time when life didn't involve this balance of public and private. Even before we met it was like this. We love living in buildings.

From here we can see six or seven other apartments well enough to know the lives of the tenants there, too. We knew the guy right across from us the best, though, but there was something weird, like he was beginning to really matter to us. Maybe it was the way he would respond to us, like with a sense of humour about the entire thing. We can see you, you can see us. We pay rent to different landlords, and we've never met, but we almost share a living room. We would talk at length about him, and we never did this about anyone else we could see, so it was strange to discover a kind of fondness growing for him. Neither of us had ever felt so involved with a stranger before and it was kind of kinky. We love kink.

There are lots of things that go on in these places that you just don't expect to be witness to. There's nothing sexy about catching sight of domestic violence, for example, or witnessing a break-in and not knowing which apartment number to tell the police. We called the police when the guy across the street died. Oh fuck, that was awful. He seemed so content, so happy. He read and did his little maps all the time. He never looked bored. But you can't always get the details right, it seems. We thought he was sleeping. For a day and a half we watched for signs of movement from him, and then we spotted the pills, the whiskey bottle on its side. Shitty. The worst part was we both began to doubt just how right we were about the people we were watching. Who knew this guy would kill himself?

We were both at work when they took his body away, and his blinds were all shut when we got back. Another person, maybe this guy's brother or lover or landlord, started cleaning up the place, putting everything in boxes. We felt sorry that we weren't actually more involved. Both of us wanted to help somehow, but it was over. This new guy never even glanced at us. It seemed like he was completely absorbed with his cleaning, but we could see him in there, talking to himself and gesturing broadly. We hate being ignored.

The apartment has only been empty for a week or two, and already someone new is moving in, but we can't tell much about him except he's kind of yuppie. One day we spotted him pulling up in a Range Rover. Disappointing. He's a complete contrast to the previous guy, and we can tell he doesn't know that someone died in his living room last month. That is a history that only we know about, and soon we will forget, too. We hate to forget.

We were watching the new guy one night. It was really stormy out. Suddenly we caught sight of this crazy-looking guy on the roof of the building. He was throwing a box of ashes from up there into the wind, frantically doing his own thing. Anyway, he looked right at us with this totally crazed look and just stood there staring. It was the weirdest thing. Neither of us had ever felt so violated by simply being seen by someone. It was really creepy so we closed the blinds. We hate closing the blinds.

12
Ashes

I *can actually feel the cells of my body flat-*
ten and compress, each one becoming a
two-dimensional form as if they were per-
ishing from cancers. I sometimes flatten out
entirely, and only there am I able to fully appre-
ciate the square, the right angle, the intersection.
It is a place that happily exists without time. I
scuttle across the floors and walls like a bead of
quicksilver, passing between the window and its
pane, out into the exterior fields of the building or
sliding into elevator shafts, beneath doors. . . . I
can explore a whole new, spatially charged uni-
verse.

– J.'s notebook

Three tablets of Flutoxocet. Wash it down with
scotch, straight from the bottle. Disapproving
stares from pedestrians as I race from my
building, out into the night, into the rain. The
bottle goes back into my bag. Something's

happening to me. I can't handle this. I rush down the block, away from something, toward something, I don't know.

The rains is coming down hard now and the wind is picking up, like a genuine gale purely for my benefit. Sheets of water sweep down the street, engulfing me and flying past. Fewer people are out in this weather, and it must be close to two in the morning anyway. A couple of brave souls walking apartment-sized dogs. I hit Barclay Street, and then turn, heading west, almost jogging. I cannot get the image of the man on the collapsing fire escape out of my mind.

The buildings are wet tonight. Trees undulate in the wind and glisten in the lamplight, making the whole world seem angry. I gaze up at the towering building at 1460 Barclay and watch it wave back and forth, a giant rubber phallus. I unzip the bag, and pry open the paint can. A handful of ashes is being thrown by the end of my arm, making a brief cloud of dust that disintegrates quickly in the rain. I try to take another swig from the scotch bottle, but most of it spills down my chin. I can't control movements so well, and I can't feel my fingers, but the whisky tastes good and braces me against the cold.

I run to 1655 Barclay, the giant bunker of a building with only one or two lit windows glimmering. Another handful of ash, this one with tiny fragments of bone, hurled out at the tower. Ripples appear as though the concrete were the surface of a pond, and the huge structure is rocking back and forth, so I think it might just fold over and crush me. I turn and run down Bidwell for a block to get out of the way of the collapsing building. Now the buildings around me are all teetering around, the parallel lines of their vertical corners curving and bending. I sense that the right angle is being mocked by the architecture itself.

Turning east onto Nelson, blocks of flats are sinking into soft earth, and people are leaping from windows and balconies. The sound of bodies slamming into the ground is all around me. I turn right down Nicola, and the street is lit by huge fires issuing from high up in the towers, the blowing branches of trees silhouetted by the flames. I hear the distinct snap of elevator cables, and the cries of whole families plummeting down shafts. One tower behind me topples over and crashes into another, and for a moment the rain is full of glass shards and shattered cement.

I disperse another fistful of J.'s remains at the corner of Pendrell, and he is lifted up into the furious wind. Some of it flies back at me, into my eyes and stinging. I run blind up Pendrell, and turn right down the hill on Broughton, running across Davie Street, startling the motorists. Debris from balconies, all the plants and chairs, fly through the air like a cartoon tornado. I take the last mouthfuls of scotch and fling the bottle up into the wind. It whistles as it spins, and continues its climb right out of sight. From Broughton, I cross Burnaby and then turn left on Harwood, not knowing, not caring where I'm going to end up.

High tension cables snap and shoot out from the floors of 1398 Harwood, falling in tangled heaps all around me. Down the corridor of the street, I can see several more buildings tip and fall towards False Creek, concrete pads caving in, and pancaking under the strain. Walls buckle and explode, and for seconds, little living rooms are visible, lit televisions tipping out into space, houseplants and furniture just sliding out and down. I stop suddenly.

I am staring up at Bay Towers, 1461 Harwood. This is where the madness all began. It still looks fairly stable, so I shatter a window in the main floor foyer with a terra cotta planter that has fallen from somewhere. The elevator is not safe, so I charge into the stairwell and begin my ascent. The stairs lead in that maddening, utilitarian rectangular spiral, every second flight a floor. Three. Four. Five. My heart is pounding like it might explode, and my manic footsteps echo in the well. The sound of the wind, too, is howling down the stairs. Seven. Eight. J.'s floor is quiet, but I pause there, looking out the hallway window at the chaos continuing all around. Buildings give up their footing and slide down the hill like cars out of control, smashing into each other, spilling their occupants across the tree-lined streets. Windows and sliding glass doors pop and burst out into space.

Back into the stairs. Nine. Ten. The door to the rooftop is locked, but I slam into it with all my weight, and it flings open, the wind and rain pouring into the vacuum of the stairwell. The wooden walkway is slick, and I brace myself against the wind, hanging on for my life to the railing. I can see huge waves on the water, crashing into the beach, and boats, loose from their moorings, being thrown up onto land. Both Nicola and Broughton have become rivers of debris and rain, and the wind carries books and photographs up over rooftops. I unzip the bag and take out the cardboard paint can. The lid comes off easily and flies away like a frisbee.

A naked man is standing at his full-length window, staring at me from the tenth floor of the building across the street. For a moment I feel like I recognize him, or that he knows me. He stares at me for only a few seconds and then explodes against the glass, spattering the window with an opaque red curtain of blood and viscera. The corners and edges of his building soften and diminish before the whole tower collapses in a flaccid heap of rubble.

I walk as close as I dare to the edge of the building and heave the can's contents out like a bucket of water. A huge cloud of ashes gets caught in the wind, and J. becomes an amorphous stream of dust, spun in the cyclone, high above the West End. The paint can falls and echoes as it hits the side of the building on its way down. I collapse. I look up, into the rain, and wipe tears and ash from my face. I am exhausted, spent, done with this task once and for all.

I pick my way back through the West End,

through the carnage of twisted metal and personal belongings. Around overturned cars and fallen trees. Bodies lay like broken dolls in the wreckage. It's like a scene from Brueghel. On the street corner a man is pulling a thick length of chain from his insides. A woman can be seen holding a dead bird at arm's length, screaming. An injured dog hurries past with the limbs of an infant clasped in its teeth. This place is a wasteland, a bomb crater, and the torrential rain can't mask the smell of death. Few buildings are still standing and even they have windows blown out, balconies hanging. One end of my own building is crushed beneath the wreckage of the neighbouring tower.

I walk like a zombie through the smashed front entrance, glass crushed underfoot in the marble foyer. In the stairwell various tenants take refuge, paralyzed with shock. I walk past and over them, and up to the third floor. They stare up at my ash-stained face and they clearly hold me responsible for all this devastation. I am completely soaked, and my feet and legs ache. I dropped the bag somewhere, but my coat is heavy with rain. The door to my apartment is ajar, and the last thing I remember is falling forward into the unlit hall.

13

#318 - 1235 Nelson Street

*A*nd I curse the moment of return to this upright, aging world. I cannot commune with this place, it is not my own. I am so out of my element here, amongst people. I belong behind the wall, under the surfaces, between the cracks. The devil's horns are not curved. They rise perfectly from his flat skull at ninety degrees from any angle in a crown of evenness.

– J.'s notebook

Morning sunlight filters in through drawn white curtains, revealing the actual weave of the cloth in a bright glow. This is a large one-bedroom with den, or that's how the landlord advertises it, but right now, the den is only being used as a sort of library. Other people would be delighted to have a two-bedroom apartment this big. In here, cases full of odd and obscure reference books line the walls, and the only other object is a large wooden chair, empty in the middle of the room. It needs mending.

Between the den and the bedroom is a lovely old-style bathroom, with beautiful black and white tiles that cover the floor and reach up the wall to the level of the frosted window. Normally, the smooth tiles are kept sparkling clean, but the tenant has allowed the place to slide recently, and there is a ring in the large, freestanding tub. The toilet bowl is stained an ugly yellow brown, and smells of algae. Flecks of toothpaste spattered and dried on the mirror above the sink. A lump of congealed shaving cream, dotted with tiny black hairs, clings to the hot water tap. The tap drips lukewarm into a bluish mineral stain.

In the hall, the hardwood floors are particularly elegant, with darker wood inlaid around the edges, and forming simple geometric patterns in every corner. The walls here are bare and white, but reflect the light through the bedroom windows with good results.

The bedroom is quite large, typical of the three-storey blocks built here in the 1930s. The light is clear and white too, adding a clean touch to the rumpled sheets on the unmade bed. Beside the bed a full ashtray lies beside a tumbler with traces of Glenlivet still inside. A well-thumbed copy of *Exercises in Style* by Raymond Queneau is just visible beneath a pillow. On the floor of the open closet is a pile of dirty laundry, much of it wet and smelling of mildew. Behind the laundry is a stack of pornographic magazines. On the wall, a small photograph of an ex-lover, dead from AIDS.

The kitchen is next down the hall, open to a large dining room/living room area. Here the same black and white tiles cover the counter surfaces, and newly-laid black and white linoleum tiles cover the floor, adding a tasteful contrast to the wood on the rest of the floors. A small island counter separates the kitchen from the space of the rest of the room, and on its top are several empty liquor bottles, bags of groceries that were never put away, and more dirty dishes that would no longer fit near the full sink. More full ash-trays. An empty pack of cigarettes. A neglected jade plant.

The curtains in the living area are drawn as well, but sealed down the middle with lengths of masking tape. The tape looks out of place and put up in questionable haste. At the large dining room table, a man in his late thirties is asleep, slumped across a mass of postcards, writings, and newspaper clippings. Some of these have been taped to the wall above the table, but unevenly and disorganized, the corners overlapping. The man is unshaven, and his greying hair is wild. Around his head and under his chair, little pools of water are shrinking in the heat of the sunlight. In front of him is a spilled bottle of anti-depressants, little round blue pills. He is fast asleep.

If you walked into this apartment, maybe being shown by the anxious landlord, you would first be delighted by the large space and its potential. But if you saw the apartment today, you would feel uneasy, like the whole space had been tainted by this man's madness. It would only take a few hours to clean the space, take the things off the walls, dispose of the rotting food and filthy ashtrays, but doing so would not clean the spirit of the rooms. Something more than the food smells here. Something is wrong with the volume of the space. Maybe if you moved in after his eviction, you would never notice it, but until then, the apartment will carry a bad vibe, like a crime scene.

The landlord is Persian, and has no interest in why his tenant lives this way. He will serve the eviction notice, and there will be shouting briefly between them, but he will get that tenant out one way or another. He has managed the building for seven years, and has seen it all. He has watched over a hundred individuals and couples move in and out of his building, and nothing surprises him anymore, but sometimes it makes him sad. He is sad to see the suffering wrought from disease. He is upset by the lack of dignity of some people, and the process of watching their lives slide away. He does not drink or smoke himself, and still observes Ramadan and Persian New Year, but his faith has weakened over the years. He has good tenants, too, and thought highly of the man in 318 until the last couple of months.

When 318 is empty, the Persian landlord will go through the motions he has come to know so well. He will ask discreetly what the prospective tenant does for a living, whether they are single, whether they like to play loud music. He will show off the space with genuine pride, warning the new person not to paint the walls. Like every other time, someone appropriate will move in and later move out, as the flow of life continues in this residential building and in the West End.

Mark Macdonald has worked in nearly every dimension of the publishing industry, from agent to bookseller to book buyer. His written work has appeared in numerous anthologies and publications. *Flat* is his first novel.

He lives in Vancouver's West End.